Samuel French Acting Edition

Heaven Help Me

by Joseph Simonelli

I0591823

‖ SAMUEL FRENCH ‖

SAMUELFRENCH.COM   SAMUELFRENCH.CO.UK

MUSIC USE NOTE

IMPORTANT BILLING AND CREDIT REQUIREMENTS

HEAVEN HELP ME was produced by Starburst Productions on August 2, 2002 at the First Avenue Playhouse, Atlantic Highlands, New Jersey. The production was directed by Joe Silk with the following cast:

RITA ROMANO . . . . Danielle Pasculli

ROLLIE HOLLOWAY . . . . James Walsh

KEVIN HOLLOWAY . . . . Joe Simonelli

SAM HOLLOWAY . . . . Gary Stern

FRED HOLLOWAY . . . . David McKirachan

MARTHA HOLLOWAY . . . . Donna Jeanne

Stage Manager - Grace Emley

CHARACTERS

ROLLIE HOLLOWAY – Late thirties. Black sheep brother.
RITA ROMANO – Mid-thirties. Rollie's latest girlfriend.
KEVIN HOLLOWAY – Early forties. Accountant, middle brother.
SAM HOLLOWAY – Mid-fifties. Older brother.
FRED HOLLOWAY – Mid-forties. Deceased brother.
MARTHAT HOLLOWAY – Late forties. Fred's widow.

SCENES

The action takes place in the Holloway beach house in Rockaway, New York.

Act One

Scene 1: Friday afternoon
Scene 2: A few minutes later

Act Two

Scene 1: Later that evening
Scene 2: Twenty minutes later
Scene 3: The next morning

ABOUT THE AUTHOR

Mr. Simonelli, a Brooklyn native, currently resides in Monmouth County, New Jersey. He is the proud father of three children, Nicholas, Kristen and Michael. In addition to writing and acting, Mr. Simonelli has been an independent Financial Advisor since 1986.

To my siblings: Claire, Phil, Artie and John (Bug)...for all the memories of the fun we had at our beach house in Breezy Point.

To my children: Nicholas, Kristen and Michael. For the memories you will always share with each other.

ACT 1

Scene One

(*SETTING: The living room of a small beach cottage in Rockaway Point, New York. A dining table is down left. A sofa is down center.*)

(*AT RISE: It is late afternoon in May. Stage is empty as we hear* **RITA ROMANO**'s *voice as she enters front door carrying two large suitcases. She is a pretty woman in her mid-thirties whose lack of higher education is well masked by her urban street smarts and sweet demeanor.*)

RITA. (*as she drops suitcases in middle of room*) Gee Rollie, the least you could've done was help me with the suitcases. (*She glances past audience through imaginary window that fronts the ocean.*) Wow, what a magnificent view. The ocean sure is beautiful, isn't it, Rollie?

(**ROLLIE** *enters behind her carrying only a small overnight bag. He is the youngest of the three surviving Holloway brothers.* **ROLLIE,** *along with* **KEVIN** *and* **SAM**, *run a chain of casual restaurants called the Luscious Onion. He is a ladies man and cad, whose only interest in the family business is dating the waitresses he's in charge of hiring.*)

ROLLIE. Yeah, except when it isn't.

RITA. Sure seems cozy. It's a shame your family is going to sell the place.

ROLLIE. What can I tell you, babe. No one uses the place anymore since my brother Fred died. My two other brothers have places of their own out on Long Island.

RITA. I prefer the Jersey shore myself. Remember, that's where we met, Rollie.

ROLLIE. *(sarcasm apparent)* That's right, you were reading palms on the boardwalk in Atlantic City. Make any money in that racket?

RITA. It had its moments.

(She strokes his lapel playfully.)

I like working for you in the restaurant better though.

ROLLIE. I recognize talent when I see it babe. That's why my brothers made me Vice President of Personnel and Forms.

RITA. Forms?

ROLLIE. Yeah forms. You know. Checks, business cards, inventory sheets. After all, you can't trust just anyone with important stuff like that.

(He moves to kiss her and she pulls away.)

RITA. We better get settled in. Oh, it's so exciting, our first trip away together...I mean besides the Holiday Inn at Kennedy airport.

(She crosses down left and enters kitchen.)

Is this the kitchen?

ROLLIE. Yeah.

(He pulls cell phone and small piece of paper from his pocket.)

RITA. *(returning to living room)* It's tiny, and dusty. Doesn't anyone cook?

ROLLIE. Martha used to. That's Fred's widow. You'll meet her later. She's coming up to sign the closing papers. *(reminiscing)* Good old Martha. She could whip up a soufflé to feed an army in forty minutes.

(He starts searching through his overnight bag.)

RITA. How long has it been since you've seen her?

ROLLIE. Not since Fred's funeral. *(He looks up from luggage.)* God, that's ten years ago. This was my parents place originally. My brothers and I spent every summer here growing up. When my Father died he left it to the four boys, but Fred and Martha were the only ones who used it. Now, since he's gone, we just decided it's time to sell.

(RITA crosses down right to observe painting hanging on wall. It is a painting of a beach house.)

RITA. Oh, I like this painting.

ROLLIE. *(glances up)* Oh yeah, nice isn't it? Fred bought that for my mother when we were kids. He said it reminded him of this beach house. It's very serene.

RITA. You think so? To me it just seems peaceful.

ROLLIE. That too.

RITA. *(crosses back to **ROLLIE** who is crouched over bag and starts to massage his shoulders)* I'd love to go to a nice little beach house like that with you, Rollie.

ROLLIE. You're in one.

RITA. I mean alone. Without all your brothers around. *(a beat)* Why don't we go away together, Rollie? Maybe a vacation to the Bahamas or someplace. Wouldn't that be romantic?

ROLLIE. I'd love to, babe, but it's our busy season. I'm swamped with work.

RITA. *(playing it up)* But Rollie, you know how I get when I'm near the ocean. The smell of the salt water just does something to me. Remember Atlantic City.

ROLLIE. *(reminiscing)* Yeah, Atlantic City.

RITA. We can play the helpless drowning victim and the hero lifeguard again...And you can be the lifeguard this time.

ROLLIE. I'm the lifeguard!

(Snapping back to reality, he continues his search.)

Nah, we couldn't. Vacations are expensive. I still haven't gotten my bonus.

RITA. The story of your life. I just don't understand it. You're a single man with no expenses who makes a decent living. What do you do with all your money?

ROLLIE. You know what a soft touch I am babe. I'm a sucker for a sob story. I keep giving my money to different charities...the Police Athletic League, the Boy Scouts...

RITA. Gambler's Anonymous.

ROLLIE. Now baby.

RITA. Unlike you Rollie, I realize the value of a dollar. I've been saving up. I'll pay for the weekend.

ROLLIE. Absolutely not, a Holloway never allows a woman to pay. We'll split it.

RITA. You mean we're really going!

ROLLIE. I get to be the lifeguard this time?

RITA. Absolutely.

ROLLIE. We'll see.

RITA. *(She hugs him.)* Oh, Rollie, you really do care.

ROLLIE. Right now, Rita my dear, all I care about is finding my shaving kit. Now, where can it be?

RITA. Maybe you left it in the car?

ROLLIE. Yeah maybe. Would you mind looking babe? I've got to make a quick call.

RITA. *(suspiciously)* To whom?

ROLLIE. *(momentarily at a loss)* Ah, my accountant.

RITA. Alright. I'll be right back.

(They motion baby kisses at each other as she exits. **ROLLIE** *dials number as door closes.)*

ROLLIE. *(He crosses to table and looks at paper. There's a deep sense of urgency as he speaks.)* Hello...hi Al, it's Rollie Holloway, can I speak to Charlie Stein please. I know he's been waiting for my call, Al. I know he's angry, he's always angry, just put him on, will you? Hello, Charlie...yeah, Charlie, you're right, Charlie, I should have called yesterday. So I'm calling today. I know, I know...I'm with my family today. I told you, we're selling the beach house, you'll get your money. My end has got to be worth a hundred-and-fifty G's. That's right, a hundred-and-fifty thou. It's a done deal. Of course, you've been patient. I know, it's my last chance, or it's out of your hands. You're a real sweetheart. Don't threaten me, Charlie, with the money I give you, I'm worth more to you alive than dead. You could milk a compulsive gambler like me at least twenty more years. Listen, third race at Belmont, number three horse. Put a hundred on the nose will you, thanks. No, I'm not just betting number three again...the horse's name is Tarot Card Reader...that's right Tarot Card Re...

(Door opens suddenly, **RITA** *is holding shaving kit.)*

RITA...my love...*(to phone)* Yes, Mr. Stein, I promise I'll have my W-2 form to you by Tuesday, we'll show that IRS, yes goodbye. *(to* **RITA***)* Accountants, they're so anal.

RITA. *(with a hint of skepticism)* Here's your shaving kit. Now remember, you promised you're going to talk to your brother Sam about transferring me to the corporate office in New York.

ROLLIE. But babe, you're doing such a great job in the Paramus store. You're already head cocktail waitress and I think you'd make a great assistant manager.

RITA. Listen Rollie, I didn't go through six years of secretarial school just to be a cocktail waitress. I gave up a promising career in Atlantic City because you told me your business offered advancement opportunities.

ROLLIE. You consider reading palms a promising career?

RITA. You forgot I was studying to be a croupier? Besides, I could be a big help at the corporate office. I'm pretty creative you know. I could design new placemats. Maybe even come up with some new items for the menu. You love my cooking, Rollie.

(He picks up overnight bag and shaving kit.)

Or at least that's what you always say. You're crazy about my rigatoni. You always say that, Rollie. Hey wait, that's a great idea for the menu.

(She motions with hand as if writing on invisible billboard.)

Rita's Rigatoni Royale...

ROLLIE. Rigatoni Royale? I don't know, it doesn't sound right. Royale is English, you need something Italian. Maybe Rigatoni Regalé Who knows, it's been a long time since I looked at my Italian grammar.

RITA. I had an Italian grandma, she died last year.

ROLLIE. Well, I walked right into that one.

RITA. What do you think Rollie? Rita's Rigatoni Regalé. It's catchy isn't it? Isn't it catchy, Rollie?

ROLLIE. I'm still not sure. I'll have to run it by Fred. He was always in charge of the menu.

RITA. I thought you told me he was dead.

(She picks up the two large suitcases.)

ROLLIE. *(He catches himself.)* Oh yeah, that's right...he's a... dead.

RITA. *(A beat, as she gives him a quizzical look.)* Come on Sir Galahad, lets get this luggage unpacked.

(They exit to bedroom as KEVIN *enters front door. He is holding a cell phone in one hand and a suitcase in the other. He is the forty-two year-old middle brother whose demeanor is the exact opposite of Rollie. As the company accountant he is all business and bottom line. He is also married to an overbearing wife to whom he is speaking when he enters.)*

KEVIN. But Susan, it's only for tonight. I'll be back first thing in the morning. I can't come home tonight, we don't know when Martha is going to arrive. Yes, dear... yes, dear, I know we have a wedding reception to go to tomorrow, I'll be home in plenty of time. What? No, we are not going out carousing tonight, we're going to sit in the cottage and play Monopoly like we do every year. I can't help it, it's a tradition.

(RITA *and* ROLLIE *reenter the room.)*

RITA. I told you I heard a voice in here.

KEVIN. I've got to go Susan. Rollic and...?

(gives ROLLIE *a quizzical look)*

ROLLIE. Rita.

KEVIN. *(with hint of disapproval)* His friend just came in.

ROLLIE. *(sarcastically in phone's direction)* Hi Susan, I won't keep him out too late tonight.

KEVIN. *(to phone)* He's teasing Susan. Yes, I'll call you in the morning. Bye.

(to ROLLIE*)*

What's the matter with you. You know how she is.

ROLLIE. Yes I know. *(spells out)* B-I-T-C-H.

KEVIN. Don't start with me again.

ROLLIE. Divorce is still legal in this state you know.

KEVIN. Sure, then she gets half of everything.

ROLLIE. *(obviously opening old wounds)* Great reason to stay in a bad marriage Kev.

RITA. *(sensing need to diffuse the situation)* Hi, I'm Rita Romano. Didn't Rollie tell you about me?

KEVIN. He might have. It's hard for me to keep track.

ROLLIE. He means keep track of all the new personnel in payroll. Kevin is our accountant.

RITA. Oh, weren't you just on the phone with him?

ROLLIE. No…no…Kevin's our corporate accountant, for the restaurants. I was on the phone with my "personal" accountant.

KEVIN. Since when do you have a personal accountant, I've been doing your taxes for years.

ROLLIE. *(to* KEVIN *with shake of head towards* RITA*)* You know Kevin, my other accountant, "Mr. Stein."

KEVIN. Oh, you mean the accountant who handles all your tax loses.

ROLLIE. That's the one.

RITA. Rollie's going to talk to your brother Sam about me working in corporate headquarters, I went through six years of school you know.

KEVIN. Really. Where, Vassar, Bryn Mawr?

RITA. Katherine Gibbs secretarial, if you don't mind.

ROLLIE. We could use some extra help at headquarters Kev. Rita's very creative.

RITA. Should I tell him about my Rigatoni idea?

KEVIN. I'd love to hear it, but I really should start unpacking.

ROLLIE. Why don't Rita and I run to the store and do a little grocery shopping. I don't imagine there's much to eat in the kitchen.

RITA. Nothing I'd put in my mouth. I'll tell you what, I'll run to the store for groceries and you two boys can discuss whatever business you have together. I gather you don't get to see much of your brother without his family around.

(She holds out her hand for money and **ROLLIE** *kisses it.)*

ROLLIE. What a girl. One in a million.

RITA. Very gallant, but I need some money.

ROLLIE. *(searching his empty pockets)* Now, let me see. I know I brought some cash.

(to **KEVIN***)*

Hey Kev, can you help me out I think I…

KEVIN. *(finishing for him again)* "…left my cash in the other jacket." You're unbelievable.

(pulls money from his pocket and hands it to **RITA***)*

I hope you know what you're getting yourself into Miss Romano.

RITA. Oh, I know exactly.

(She kisses **ROLLIE** *on the cheek and exits.)*

KEVIN. You sure can pick 'em Rollie.

ROLLIE. Don't start with me.

KEVIN. *(starts to pace as* **ROLLIE** *opens a newspaper and starts to handicap horse races)* Do you realize what dire straights our company is in right now.

(sees that **ROLLIE** *is oblivious)*

KEVIN. No, you don't do you. We've been bleeding red ink for seven years and all you can think about is women and gambling. What's that your reading?

ROLLIE. The racing form.

KEVIN. *(exasperated)* The racing form? Playboy Rollie. He fiddles while Rome burns.

ROLLIE. *(unconcerned)* Relax will you. The restaurants will survive. We've been in trouble before and always pulled out of it.

KEVIN. No thanks to you, Rollie.

ROLLIE. Don't start blaming me Kev, you and Sammy run the show, I'm merely window dressing.

KEVIN. Oh yeah Mr. "Vice President of Personnel." By the way, the prices on the last menu came out backwards again.

ROLLIE. You know I'm dyslexic.

KEVIN. Never mind that.

(pulling a report from his briefcase)

Here, look at this. The profit and loss for the Luscious Onion chain of restaurants. New York State, out of twelve stores, only five are making money. Connecticut, eight stores, three are profitable and Jersey...

ROLLIE. *(still disinterested)* What about Jersey?

KEVIN. In Jersey out of six stores only one is making money!

ROLLIE. *(finally, looking up as his interest is piqued)* Really, which one?

KEVIN. Paramus.

ROLLIE. *(proud of himself)* I knew it. That's because I hired Rita for that store. What a gal.

KEVIN. I seem to recall that you hire waitresses for all the stores. And most of them are losing money. What's your excuse for that?

ROLLIE. *(now up and walking around)* I'm working on it. You think girls like Rita grow on trees? It takes months of painstaking interviews before I find women with the right qualifications.

KEVIN. *(exasperated)* Right qualifications! You're the only personnel director I know who hires on looks. This isn't a modeling agency or an escort service.

ROLLIE. The waitresses have to look nice for the customers, don't they?

KEVIN. They also have to know how to read the menus and

write the orders down.

ROLLIE. Listen Kev, the problem with the restaurants is not the staff and you know it. If Fred were still alive...

KEVIN. Well he's not.

ROLLIE. Yeah, he's not. Except for every May 15th.

KEVIN. Don't start with that.

(walks to bar and starts to examine liquor bottles)

ROLLIE. You think he'll show up tonight?

KEVIN. *(pouring a drink)* I don't want to talk about it.

ROLLIE. Why not, he's shown up the last ten years, only stands to reason...

KEVIN. *(sips drink and gags as he examines the bottle)* Yuck, I thought scotch didn't go bad. Listen, I'm still not convinced of what happened the last ten years. It seems like a bad dream. And don't go bringing it up to Sam either. You know he thinks we're crazy.

ROLLIE. Sam's in denial. Always has been. First when Mom and Pop died, and now Fred.

(He pours drink from same bottle and downs it without incident as **KEVIN** *watches.)*

KEVIN. That didn't taste funny to you?

ROLLIE. Delicious. You just don't appreciate aged scotch.

(He pours another glass.)

KEVIN. In any case, don't go bringing up Fred to Sam. He's under enough pressure.

ROLLIE. *(He sips drink and sits back down with racing form.)* We're all under pressure.

KEVIN. Yeah, but Sam especially. You know how he feels about being the oldest. He'll do anything to save the restaurants. He's sentimental about the family. The only reason he agreed to sell this house is because he's putting his share of the money back into the business. He even blames himself for Fred.

ROLLIE. Fred's death was not his fault.

KEVIN. I know Rollie. But Sam gave him the night off ten years ago and he feels responsible. But how would you remember. You were away living the high life in Las Vegas, while the rest of us were working our butts off in the restaurants.

ROLLIE. I flew right back from Vegas when I heard about Fred. Besides, I've been here ever since haven't I?

KEVIN. That doesn't make up for Fred. Or for the way Sam feels.

ROLLIE. Well, then Sam better begin to let go.

KEVIN. Of what?

ROLLIE. Of his guilty conscience. That's what. Fred's death, this beach house, even the restaurants.

KEVIN. He'll never give up the business. Even if it kills him.

ROLLIE. And it probably will.

KEVIN. Don't make light of it. Sam is losing it. Haven't you noticed that he's been acting a little strange lately?

ROLLIE. Not really, he seems perfectly fine to me.

KEVIN. What do you know. You're never in the office. And when you are you're just taking the secretaries to lunch.

ROLLIE. People have to eat.

KEVIN. Look Rollie, I'm being serious here. I work closely with Sam every day, and I'm telling you the pressure's getting to him. He's cracking up.

ROLLIE. You're imagining things.

(Door opens suddenly and SAM *enters wearing a loud Hawaiian shirt and sombrero, carrying a ukulele and a Monopoly game.)*

SAM. I've got the Monopoly set! Let's get cracking boys!

(blackout)

Scene Two

(Ten minutes later. The three men are playing Monopoly. A song like Glenn Miller's "String of Pearls" is playing on the radio.)

KEVIN. *(rolling dice)* Look Sam, maybe we should skip Monopoly and just talk business this year.

SAM. Never. Monopoly's been a tradition in this house since the game was invented. Your grandfather Holloway used to play it at this very table before any of us were born.

ROLLIE. He's right, Kev. We have to play the game.

KEVIN. Alright, but we're not playing with real money this year.

ROLLIE. You take the fun out of everything.

SAM. What's with the ancient music?

KEVIN. I had the movers pack up all the valuable stuff. I just left that old radio. They'll come for the furniture tomorrow.

ROLLIE. The problem is the radio only gets one station. Nostalgia.

(As they play the game SAM looks up and notices the picture of the beach house. The song on the radio changes something in the style of Sinatra's "Witchcraft."*)

SAM. *(to KEVIN)* I thought you said you packed away all the valuables.

KEVIN. So?

SAM. What about the picture?

(KEVIN looks to ROLLIE.)

ROLLIE. Well Sam, we kind of thought the picture should stay with the house. You know, for him.

SAM. *(terse)* He's dead. He doesn't need it.

KEVIN. Still and all Sam, it has no monetary value. Let it stay with the house.

*Please see "Music Use Note" on page three.

SAM. Alright, let it stay already.

(getting ready to roll dice)

Would somebody turn that music down, I can't hear myself think.

ROLLIE. It's Sinatra Sammy, you love Sinatra.

SAM. I know, but not so loud. I have to concentrate on a seven to hit Boardwalk. Seven, seven, seven, seven.

(He rolls.)

KEVIN. Six, Luxury Tax. Seventy-five bucks. Hand it over.

SAM. Damn. I told you the music's too loud.

ROLLIE. *(gets up to turn down music)* Don't ever play craps in Atlantic City. Seventy-five bucks. Put it in the middle.

KEVIN. It goes to the bank, not in the middle.

SAM. Kevin's right, it goes to the bank.

ROLLIE. It does not. It goes in the middle and whoever lands on Free Parking gets the dough.

KEVIN. That's not what the rules say.

ROLLIE. Screw the rules. *(to KEVIN)* And how come you're always the banker.

SAM. He's good with numbers, he's the banker.

ROLLIE. Says who.

SAM. Says me.

KEVIN. I've always been the banker, since we were kids.

ROLLIE. And since we've been kids, we've always put the money in the middle for Free Parking.

KEVIN. It ruins the integrity of the game. The whole game is based on the struggle to build from nothing and see who survives. Just like the real world. In the real world no one just hands out money.

ROLLIE. Yeah, what about hitting the lottery?

SAM. *(sarcastically)* Or a trifecta.

ROLLIE. Don't you start with me Sam.

SAM. You gamble too much, Roland. The loan sharks are always chasing you. Remember when they beat you up and you spent three months in the hospital?

ROLLIE. So what?

SAM. So, it's not right. Mom and Pop raised you better than that.

ROLLIE. Get off my back Sam. Who died and left you boss anyway?

SAM. Pop did. That's who.

ROLLIE. *(sarcastically)* Pop did, that's who.

KEVIN. Would you two cut it out. You're acting like children for Pete's sake. Now, act like adults...and play Monopoly.

SAM. It's his fault, he never listens. I try to give him good sound advice but he never listens.

ROLLIE. And I still don't see why Kevin always gets to be banker. Give me one good reason why he should always be banker?

SAM. He's an accountant and I can't trust you with money.

ROLLIE. I only asked for one good reason.

KEVIN. *(exasperated)* I get to be banker because ever since you came along you got to be the racing car.

SAM. *(to KEVIN)* He's the youngest, he gets his choice.

KEVIN. *(standing up.)* There you see, just like when Pop was alive. "He's the baby, let him have his way."

ROLLIE. *(calmly imitating a Viennese therapist)* Aha, zee middle child syndrome, I must consult with Herr Dr. Freud about this case.

SAM. Keep quiet Roland, your brother's right, it's time you were more responsible.

KEVIN. Yeah, no more coddling. If you don't start pulling your weight around the office we can kiss the restaurants goodbye. We're barely hanging on by a thread now. You can't expect Sam and I to keep carrying the load forever.

SAM. Listen Kevin, we are not going to lose the business. Not after all Pop did to start those restaurants.

KEVIN. I brought the figures with me. I'll be glad to show them to you.

SAM. Never mind the figures. I'll think of something. I always do. *(to* **ROLLIE***)* And Kevin's right, Roland. It's time you started to pull your own weight.

KEVIN. I told you Rollie, it's time to face the music...

SAM. *(stands, suddenly excited)* That's it. Music!

ROLLIE. What are you talking about?

SAM. Quiet, I'm having a creative jag.

(He frantically runs to pick up the ukulele as if in a maniacal trance.)

We have theme music nights in all the restaurants. Friday is Hawaiian night. A Luau, roasted pigs, and Hawaiian music. *(He starts to pluck and sing a Hawaiian style song.)*

*(***RITA*** enters the room carrying a grocery bag as* **ROLLIE** *jumps up, takes the bag from her and places sombrero on her head as she starts to dance.)*

ROLLIE. Yeah! Yeah! I can see it now. We dress the waitresses in grass skirts and they greet the customers with a flowered necklace.

RITA. Lei?

ROLLIE. Not now, babe, I'm busy.

RITA. No, the flowered necklace, it's called a lei.

*(***SAM*** starts to dance with* **RITA** *as* **ROLLIE** *continues to strum.)*

SAM. Hello girlie, I'm Sam.

RITA. Pleased to meet you. I'm Rita, Rollie's friend.

KEVIN. *(He can stand no more.)* Wait a minute! Wait a minute! Are you all nuts. Am I the only sane person in the room. It's like being trapped on a sinking ship, running to get the Captain and finding out he's Daffy Duck.

SAM. Who's Daffy Duck?

KEVIN. You are Sam. And this guy's Bugs Bunny *(He looks at* **RITA***.)* and you...you...I don't know who you are.

RITA. I'm Rita, did you forget already?

KEVIN. *(hand to forehead)* Heaven help me.

ROLLIE. Lighten up, will you Kevin, you're way too tense. *(to RITA)* Why don't you put the groceries away babe. We've got to finish the game.

RITA. Okay, sweetie. I like your family. Don't forget to talk to you know who.

(She exits to the kitchen with groceries as the three men return to their seats to continue the game.)

SAM. Now, who's turn was it?

KEVIN. My turn.

ROLLIE. No, it was my turn.

KEVIN. No, Sam just rolled and landed on Luxury Tax remember.

ROLLIE. *(getting louder)* That's right, put the money on Free Parking.

KEVIN. *(just as loud)* It goes to the bank.

(An argument ensues.)

ROLLIE. Free Parking!

KEVIN. Bank!

ROLLIE. Free Parking!

KEVIN. B-A-N-K Bank!

SAM. *(standing)* Would you two knock it off, you'll wake the dead!

(Suddenly the lights flicker and a song in the vien of "That Old Black Magic" begins to play on the radio.* This is Fred's theme music, it plays whenever he appears onstage. FRED enters from bedroom door as music fades. He is apparently only visible to Rollie and Kevin.)

FRED. Hey guys, what's with all the shouting, you woke me up from a dead sleep.

ROLLIE. He's here again.

KEVIN. I see.

SAM. Who's here?

FRED. Wow, Monopoly. Can I play?

*Please see "Music Use Note" on page three.

KEVIN. No you can't.

SAM. Can't what?

ROLLIE. Can't play Monopoly.

SAM. I most certainly can.

KEVIN. *(to SAM)* Not you...him.

SAM. Who?

ROLLIE. Fred.

SAM. FRED!

FRED. Why can't I play?

(KEVIN *and* ROLLIE *look at each other having been through the situation before.)*

KEVIN. Because, you're dead, Fred.

FRED. I am not.

ROLLIE. Yes, you are, Fred.

SAM. *(stands and starts to pace)* Oh no, don't start that nonsense again. Every year the same thing. You two think you see our dead brother. The joke's getting worn.

FRED. I don't feel very dead.

KEVIN. Take our word for it. You are.

FRED. Prove it.

KEVIN. Prove it! *(He shrugs and looks at* ROLLIE.*)* Prove it.

ROLLIE. Prove it?

SAM. Now, cut this stuff out!

ROLLIE. Okay, Fred. I'll ask you some questions. You've been dead ten years. I'll ask you some questions about recent events that you couldn't possibly know.

FRED. Ask away.

SAM. I know what this is. *(He points to* KEVIN.*)* This is your doing. It's a conspiracy. You two want to drive me crazy then have me declared incompetent so you can sell the business out from under me.

KEVIN. That's ridiculous, Sam. Fred's standing right there as plain as day.

ROLLIE. First question. Who won the World Series last year?

FRED. *(without missing a beat)* The Yankees.

ROLLIE. *(shaking his head)* Bad question. They win every year.

SAM. You're not gonna get away with this.

(He walks towards the kitchen.)

KEVIN. Where are you going?

SAM. To the kitchen. To talk to a real person

ROLLIE. We're not trying to pull a fast one Sam. Fred is here.

SAM. And you. Instead of gambling and talking to dead people why don't you come up with an idea for the restaurants.

ROLLIE. *(indignant)* I've come up with some terrific ideas for the restaurant and you never use them.

SAM. Terrific ideas? *(to KEVIN)* His last terrific idea was free entrée night.

ROLLIE. It brought people in.

SAM. I've got to make a phone call. You want to ask our dead brother questions? Ask him what we should do to increase business because if we don't we'll be joining him soon. We'll all starve to death.

(He's off in a huff.)

FRED. Why's Sam so upset? And why won't he talk to me?

KEVIN. He won't talk to because he can't see you, because you're dead. A ghost, a metaphysical spirit wrought into being, and apparent only to us for some unknown reason.

FRED. *(sitting on couch)* He sees me alright. And I'm not dead.

(KEVIN and ROLLIE look at each. ROLLIE sits next to FRED.)

FRED. I'm not really dead. Am I Rollie?

ROLLIE. *(with pity)* I'm afraid so, kid. You died ten years ago.

FRED. *(rises)* But it can't be. It just can't be. Ask me one more question Rollie. *(pleading)* Kevin, ask me just one more question.

KEVIN. *(nodding to* **ROLLIE***)* Go ahead, ask.

ROLLIE. Who's President of the United States?

FRED. That's easy, George Bush.

KEVIN. Junior or senior?

FRED. *(collapses on couch)* Junior or senior? I really am dead.

KEVIN. We tried to tell you Fred.

> *(pause)*

FRED. Well, somebody say something.

ROLLIE. You look good. For someone your age.

FRED. Ten years. That means I'm…

KEVIN. Fifty six.

FRED. How did it happen? How did I die?

> *(Again* **KEVIN** *looks at* **ROLLIE** *as music rises.)*

KEVIN. You went swimming. Ten years ago tonight. We were all here playing Monopoly. It was a hot night for May, just like tonight.

FRED. I drowned? But I'm a good swimmer, you know that Rollie, I've been swimming that beach since I was a kid.

ROLLIE. There was a bad rip tide that night kid. They never…well…

FRED. What? Never what?

KEVIN. They never found your body, Freddy.

FRED. *(***FRED** *lowers his head momentarily, then looks up.)* Martha! How's my wife?

ROLLIE. She's fine kid, just fine. As a matter of fact she's coming here tonight to…

> *(***KEVIN** *shakes his head to stop* **ROLLIE***.)*

FRED. To what?

KEVIN. To visit, Fred, to visit.

FRED. Wow, I'm gonna see Martha again. Gee, I miss her, just thinking about her makes me feel better.

ROLLIE. There's one more thing kid.

FRED. Yeah.

ROLLIE. Well Martha is kind of, well…remarried.

FRED. Remarried?

ROLLIE. To a wealthy stockbroker. We've been telling you for the last three years. I wish you'd process the information already.

FRED. I don't understand.

KEVIN. It's like this, Fred. Every year for the last ten years you show up here and Rollie and I have to convince you that you're dead. Three years ago your widow got remarried.

FRED. So soon?

KEVIN. She waited seven years, Fred. It's not like you were separated and were going to reconcile some day. You're dead, pal. She hasn't been back to this house since you died.

FRED. *(slumps down in wing chair, so as to be hidden from behind)* Gee, I guess you're right.

(Door opens and **MARTHA** *appears. She greets* **KEVIN** *and* **ROLLIE** *then notices* **FRED.** *)*

MARTHA. Hi Kevin, Rollie, Fred…FRED!

(She faints onto couch.)

ROLLIE. *(as he and* **KEVIN** *rush to the couch)* So much for reunions.

KEVIN. Martha speak to us.

FRED. Gee, I didn't mean to frighten her.

ROLLIE. *(as he checks her over)* She's out cold.

FRED. She doesn't look so good.

KEVIN. Of course not. She just fainted.

FRED. I mean she looks different Her hair, she looks, well…

ROLLIE. Older?

FRED. Well, yeah.

KEVIN. Don't forget Fred, you remember her from ten years ago.

FRED. Oh, yeah. I guess you're right. Ah, but it's still great to see her.

ROLLIE. She only came back tonight because...*(He looks at* KEVIN.*)* Well, we're selling the house Fred. I don't know any other way to say it.

FRED. *(confused)* Selling the house? You can't Rollie. You can't be serious. *(to* KEVIN*)* Kevin, you can't sell the house.

KEVIN. I'm afraid it's already done. The buyer's coming tonight. That's why Martha is here. To sign the closing papers.

FRED. But why? Why sell the beach house?

KEVIN. No one uses it anymore since...you know.

ROLLIE. Besides, we can use the money. For the business. The restaurants are in bad shape, aren't they, Kev?

FRED. *(on to* ROLLIE*)* Oh, I see. It's not the business. You need money again, don't you Rollie? You aren't still gambling, are you? Pop never liked gamblers. You could get hurt again. You could wind up...like me.

ROLLIE. Great, it's not bad enough I get it from the two live ones, now I have Marley's ghost lecturing me.

FRED. You can't sell the house. Just think of all the memories we've had here. Pop barbecuing in the back yard. Mom watering that big hydrangea bush in the garden. Remember how she loved that garden.

KEVIN. Yeah, I remember. Then we'd be all sweaty from playing volleyball on the beach and Mom would make us a big pitcher of lemonade.

FRED. And Rollie and Sam would always fight to see who got to help Pop flip the hamburgers. So many memories. And Kevin, you first kissed your wife right out on the porch late one summer night.

ROLLIE. I bet he wished he hadn't.

FRED. Yeah Kev, you kissed Susan right there and me and Rollie were spying on you from the window in the kitchen. Remember Rollie?

ROLLIE. *(sarcastically)* Cut it out Fred, you're breaking my heart.

KEVIN. Now, you don't have to be nasty to Fred, Rollie.

ROLLIE. Nasty to Fred. Are you kidding? I'm being nasty to a figment of my imagination. We're both probably just having a mass hallucination. *(to* FRED*)* What are you even doing here? Shouldn't you be on some cloud somewhere playing a harp?

FRED. I don't know what I'm doing here, Rollie. I don't know what I'm doing here any more than you do. All I remember is darkness, as if I'm sleeping. And not the kind of sleeping where you dream about something, just pitch blackness. Than I'm wakened by the sound of you guys playing Monopoly and I come in from my room to find you.

ROLLIE. Well, I don't think this is where you're supposed to be.

FRED. How do you know Rollie? How do you know where I should be? Remember Pop's nickname for this house.

KEVIN. Holloway Heaven.

FRED. Well, maybe this is exactly where I'm supposed to be.

ROLLIE. I'm sorry Fred, but what's done is done. The house is sold and that's that.

FRED. But if the house is sold, then what's going to happen to me? Kevin, what's going to happen to me?

KEVIN. *(shaking his head)* I don't know Freddy.

FRED. I've got to go figure this out.

(Fred's theme music comes up, FRED *exits the same way he entered, and music fades out.)*

KEVIN. You didn't have to be so blunt with him. You know he's sensitive.

ROLLIE. Was sensitive you mean. Alright, I'm sorry.

KEVIN. Well, we've got to do something for him. We can't just leave him like this. You're the fast thinking, smooth talking man of the world. Can't you think of a way to help him?

ROLLIE. Help him what? Get to heaven? Listen to yourself! You think I'm up on the latest ghost rules? What do I know? Try an exorcism!

(KEVIN's cell phone starts ringing as the picture of the beach house falls off the wall. ROLLIE walks over, picks it up and places it on table.)

ROLLIE. How'd that happen?

KEVIN. *(to cell phone)* Hello? Yes, this is he. Oh, hello, we've been expecting you...oh, I see. Yes, I understand. Of course, it's unavoidable, yes. I'll try, but a prime piece of real estate like this won't last long. We've had quite a few other offers and...okay, but I can't make any promises.

ROLLIE. *(a little concerned)* Who was that?

KEVIN. Our buyer. Bad news.

ROLLIE. Don't tell me.

KEVIN. His mortgage commitment fell through. Something about his ex-wife garnishing his salary.

ROLLIE. This is terrible.

KEVIN. I can't understand it. The deal was all set. Hey, you don't think?

(He takes the picture from ROLLIE.)

ROLLIE. Fred? Come on, don't be ridiculous.

KEVIN. What about this?

(He holds up picture.)

ROLLIE. It slipped off the nail, that's all. Gimmee that. *(He re-hangs picture.)*

KEVIN. Bit of a coincidence. Wouldn't you say.

ROLLIE. Never mind that. What are we gonna do now. You do have back-up buyers for this place, don't you?

KEVIN. Not for the price he was paying. I was just feeding him a line to keep him interested.

ROLLIE. Well, we'll just have to take less. I was counting on that money.

KEVIN. For what? Oh, I get it...Mr. Stein. How much are you in to him for this time?

(ROLLIE sits at table and buries his head in his hands as RITA enters carrying crackers.)

ROLLIE. I'm getting a headache. That's how much.

KEVIN. *(pointing his finger at him)* I told you. I told you.

ROLLIE. *(nodding head towards* **RITA***)* Shush.

RITA. Anybody want a Ritz?

KEVIN & ROLLIE. No.

RITA. Who's on the couch?

KEVIN. Martha.

RITA. Oh, that's Martha. She doesn't look so good.

KEVIN. We know.

RITA. She must have had a long trip to be so tired already. Shouldn't she be napping in the bedroom instead of on the couch?

ROLLIE. She's not napping. She fainted when she saw...

KEVIN. *(interrupting and finishing)* The décor. She's funny that way. Very fashion conscious. We painted the whole place over and the poor girl took one look at the wall color and passed out. She was expecting seafoam green with a magenta border.

RITA. No kidding. I kind of like the color. *(She crosses behind* **ROLLIE.***)* What's the matter baby?

ROLLIE. I've got a splitting headache.

RITA. Where?

ROLLIE. In my head.

RITA. I mean what part?

KEVIN. The empty part.

ROLLIE. Right on my forehead.

RITA. It's probably just sinuses. I have a good cure for that. I just tap your forehead to relieve the pressure. Like this.

(She starts tapping his forehead with her fingers.)

Now how does that feel?

KEVIN. Hit him harder.

RITA. You see, if I keep tapping your head I'll loosen your sinuses.

ROLLIE. Are you trying to loosen 'em or kill 'em.

*(***MARTHA** *starts to moan as* **SAM** *enters.)*

KEVIN. She's coming to.

(He crosses to couch.)

SAM. What's going on here. What happened to Martha?

KEVIN. She fainted when she saw...

SAM. Don't say it.

KEVIN. You know who.

SAM. Cut it out.

RITA. Who's you know who?

ROLLIE. *(rising from table)* FRED. FRED. FRED. There I said it Sam.

(**MARTHA** *starts to regain consciousness as* **KEVIN** *helps her sit up.)*

RITA. I thought Fred was dead?

SAM. He is.

ROLLIE. Is not.

SAM. Is.

MARTHA. Oh, my goodness.

SAM. Are you all right dear.

MARTHA. Oh, Sam, Kevin. I had the weirdest dream. What happened to me?

RITA. You fainted when you saw your dead husband.

MARTHA. Oh, my... *(She starts to sway again.)*

KEVIN. *(holding her up)* It's okay. Relax.

MARTHA. But, what that...*(She looks at* **RITA** *distastefully.)* woman said.

RITA. *(trying to impress her)* I'm RITA, Rollie's fiancée.

ROLLIE. FIANCÉE!

RITA. Well, practically.

SAM. Everything is fine dear. It's just the shock of coming back here to the house again after so many years. All the memories.

ROLLIE. *(walks to her)* Hello, Martha. It's good to see you again.

MARTHA. Oh, hello Roland. *(She looks at* **RITA**.*)* Congratulations. I think. You haven't set a date yet, have you?

ROLLIE. *(Tongue in cheek, as he tries to save face for **RITA**.)* Next January, weather permitting.

MARTHA. Thank God for that. It will give you ample time to...to think about it.

*(**RITA** makes a move towards her, but **ROLLIE** intercepts her.)*

ROLLIE. Rita, why don't you fix Martha a cup of tea.

MARTHA. No tea, I think I need a stiff drink.

*(**KEVIN** and **ROLLIE** look at each other.)*

RITA. *(Seething, she makes a fist.)* I'd like to give her something stiff.

KEVIN. Well, all we have is some pretty old scotch, but I...

MARTHA. That will do fine.

*(**KEVIN** starts mixing a drink for **MARTHA**.)*

ROLLIE. *(trying to diffuse the tension)* Come on Rita dear. Let's go check to see if the hedges need trimming.

RITA. This house doesn't have hedges.

ROLLIE. Than we'll plant some. See you later folks.

*(**ROLLIE** ushers **RITA** out the front door.)*

MARTHA. *(rises from couch and crosses to table)* You boys are still playing Monopoly I see. *(She looks at picture.)* Fred's picture. Oh, how he loved it. I just can't believe we're finally letting go of the house.

KEVIN. *(handing her the drink)* Well, we're not exactly letting go yet.

SAM. What do you mean?

KEVIN. The buyer called. He's backing out.

SAM. Backing out?

MARTHA. You're kidding.

KEVIN. It's true. Sorry to have dragged you out here for nothing Martha.

SAM. But I was depending on that money.

KEVIN. Look, I'll try to find another buyer as soon as I can.

SAM. But you don't understand...

(He looks at **MARTHA** *as she downs her drink.)*

Kevin, do you mind if Martha and I have a private conversation.

KEVIN. Be my guest. I have some calls to make. That scotch taste okay to you Martha?

MARTHA. Delicious.

*(***KEVIN*** goes off to bedroom shaking his head.)*

SAM. Can I get you another drink, Martha dear?

MARTHA. Please do.

*(***MARTHA*** hands him her glass and he refills it, as Fred's theme music comes up. ***FRED*** enters the room and stands in bedroom doorway, silently reacting to all that is said.)*

SAM. I'm sorry for the inconvenience, Martha. For having you fly all the way from California for nothing. I'm sure we'll get another buyer soon.

MARTHA. Let's hope so. By the way Sam, I do hope you're going to convince Roland not to marry that woman.

SAM. Why. She seems like a nice gal.

MARTHA. I just think he can do better, that's all.

(He hands her the drink.)

SAM. You mean like you did, marrying that stockbroker.

*(***FRED*** shakes his head slowly.)*

MARTHA. I don't think I like the tone of that remark.

SAM. I'm sorry if it sounded insensitive. Please forgive me… *(raising glass)* for old times' sake?

MARTHA. Okay. For old times' sake. Speaking of which, I hear through the grapevine that the restaurants are foundering like the Titanic.

SAM. Must be a pretty long vine reaching all the way to Malibu.

MARTHA. Come now, Sam, there's no denying it. After all I still own Fred's twenty-five percent. Do you think I don't check up on things.

*(***SAM*** sits on couch.)*

SAM. So, who spilled the beans?

MARTHA. I'll give you a hint. It was one of your brothers, and not the one who drinks, gambles and chases floozies.

SAM. Kevin.

MARTHA. Don't point fingers. He's only doing what's proper and expected of a good accountant.

SAM. Yeah, well sometimes I wish he'd be a little less diligent.

MARTHA. Oh, Sam, when are you going to give in and sell the restaurants while there's still something left to sell?

SAM. *(jumps up)* Sell the Luscious Onion chain? My father's life work? Never!

MARTHA. Come on, Sam! The success of that restaurant died with your brother, my late husband. Whatever magic your father had managing restaurants was passed on to Fred. When he died, so did the formula for success. Let's face it. He picked the right locations, the right menu's…it's a testament to his ability that the business lasted ten years after he's gone.

*(**FRED** nonchalantly cups his right hand, blows on fingers and rubs them on his lapel as if his achievements were nothing.)*

SAM. Alright, he was a restaurant genius like Pop. But what do you want me to do, give up?

*(**FRED** shakes his head in support of **SAM**.)*

MARTHA. Precisely, give up.

SAM. You know I can't do that.

MARTHA. I'm afraid you're going to have to.

SAM. But Martha, if you could just lend me some money that would be enough to keep us afloat until I can straighten things out.

MARTHA. Lend you the money? Ha! That, is a laugh Sam.

SAM. Well, why not. You made a good living off that business when my brother was alive. It bought you a nice home in New Jersey. Beautiful clothes, fancy cars…

MARTHA. Believe me Sam, I would love to lend you the money, but for one small fact.

SAM. And what would that be?

MARTHA. There is no money, Sam.

SAM. What?

MARTHA. It's all gone. Poof!

SAM. But how? You married that stockbroker. Moved to Malibu.

MARTHA. Oh, it's a funny thing about my soon-to-be former husband.

SAM. You're getting divorced?

(FRED *gives the thumbs up sign.*)

MARTHA. Seems I trusted one husband too many. *(beat)* Your brother was a good-hearted, generous person. I never doubted his integrity and always did as he told me with money. I'm afraid I wasn't so lucky with my present spouse. It seems he got involved in a stock scandal involving some utility company on the coast. He lost most of what we had and the rest of our holdings are being frozen to pay of the investors he bilked.

SAM. But Martha, you had your own assets going into the marriage. Everything you and Fred worked for.

MARTHA. All gone Sam. He conned me out of everything, just the way he did his clients. He told me he'd triple my money in the stock market, and well, we know how that turned out. I don't think it would sit right – me being the wife of a convict – so I'm divorcing him and moving on with my life.

SAM. I can't believe it.

MARTHA. Oh, it's all true, Sam. So you see, the only sensible thing to do is for us to sell this house as soon as possible, then liquidate the business.

SAM. I told you, I will never sell those restaurants.

MARTHA. I'm afraid you won't have much choice Sam. It will be three against one.

SAM. My brothers will never go against me.

MARTHA. Sam, you are such a cockeyed optimist. Think about it, Sam, how hard do you think it would be for me to convince Kevin's wife to take the money and run? After all, Sam, Kevin's a CPA and a very practical man. He could easily land another job with a more stable organization. He has a family to think about.

SAM. Well, you won't turn Roland. Blood is thicker than water you know.

MARTHA. Oh, you mean Rollie the ne'er-do-well black sheep of the family? I would imagine that he probably owes a good sum of money to some shady character, and he doesn't have you or the business to borrow it from anymore. That is, unless you're going to tell me that the leopard has changed his spots in the last ten years.

SAM. I can't believe my brother married such a devious woman.

MARTHA. Not devious, Sam, desperate. That's a lot worse. I'm afraid your dear departed brother took such great care of me, that I've grown quite accustomed to the good things in life, and I'm not quite so ready to give them up.

SAM. I warn you, Martha. I'm not giving up without a fight.

MARTHA. Fight all you want, Sam, but what I'm doing is for everyone's good and you know it.

(**FRED** *shakes his head and walks off to bedroom as door opens and* **RITA** *enters with* **ROLLIE** *behind her. He is sporting a black eye.*)

RITA. I'll try and find some ice.

SAM. What happened to him?

RITA. He ran into one of his old cronies on the boardwalk. They started arguing, and the next thing I know, they're tussling on the ground.

(*She exits for ice.*)

SAM. (*yells*) Kevin, get in here! (*to* **ROLLIE**) Who'd you run into?

ROLLIE. Johnny Sims. He owes me money from a bet and he wouldn't pay up.

SAM. Johnny Sims! That psycho. When's the last time you saw him?

ROLLIE. I think it was the late eighties.

(*KEVIN enters.*)

SAM. The late eighties! You're trying to collect on a bet you made over twenty years ago?

ROLLIE. A bet's a bet. That lousy welcher.

KEVIN. What happened to your eye?

(*RITA enters holding towel.*)

RITA. He won a bet.

KEVIN. What?

RITA. You should see the other guy.

MARTHA. So, we're all finally here. It's just as well. I think we all need to have a talk.

ROLLIE. About what?

MARTHA. Selling this house and liquidating the business.

(*The picture again falls from wall, accompanied by a loud tapping on wall.*)

RITA. How'd that happen?

MARTHA. That's strange.

KEVIN. I think it's you-know-who again.

ROLLIE. I think he's angry. I'd tone down the selling the house rhetoric.

MARTHA. You mean it's Fred?

KEVIN. It ain't House & Garden.

(*It is quiet again.*)

MARTHA. Well, what do we do?

ROLLIE. We better try to contact him.

SAM. That's crazy talk.

MARTHA. And how would we contact him?

KEVIN. I don't know. Usually he just shows up.

RITA. Why don't we have a séance?

ROLLIE. What do we know about having a séance?

RITA. I bet I could do it.

ROLLIE. What, you read a few palms in Atlantic City so that qualifies you as a medium?

MARTHA. She looks more like a large to me.

(*RITA lunges towards* **MARTHA** *again as* **SAM** *and* **KEVIN** *intercept her.*)

SAM. Calm down.

KEVIN. Easy now.

RITA. One day, no one's gonna be there to hold me back.

SAM. Would you two cut it out.

ROLLIE. So it's settled. We have a séance to try and contact Fred.

SAM. I told you that's crazy.

KEVIN. Rollie's right, it's the only way.

SAM. You're nuts, too.

KEVIN. I'll tell you what then, Sam. Maybe you can show this house to prospective buyers and when Fred goes into his ghost of Christmas past routine you can explain the pictures falling and tapping noises.

SAM. You may have a point.

RITA. If only we had a sign.

(*using her best "mystic" voice*)

Spirit of Fred. Spirit of Fred. If you would like us to try and contact you please give us a sign.

(*Full special effects: radio blasts Fred's theme music lights flicker, tapping on walls, doors swing open, wind sounds etc.*)

RITA. I'll take that as a yes.

(*curtain*)

ACT II

Scene One

(AT RISE: It is later that evening. All are seated around table. The house lights are dim as a candle burns on top of Monopoly board which is still set up. RITA sits center with ROLLIE to her right, and KEVIN to her left. MARTHA is right of Rollie, and SAM left of Kevin.)

ROLLIE. You really think this will work, huh?

(Unless otherwise specified, RITA speaks in a mystical chanting voice.)

RITA. You must remain perfectly quiet while I try to contact the spirit world. Now, I want all gathered around this table to join hands. *(normal voice)* That's not my hand, Rollie.

ROLLIE. Sorry, babe.

SAM. This is the most idiotic thing I've ever done.

RITA. Silence, or you will break the spell. The spirits are restless tonight.

SAM. The only spirits around here are in that scotch bottle behind me.

RITA. You must do exactly as I say. I am about to put myself into a hypnotic trance.

MARTHA. *(mimicking Rita's 'chanting' voice)* How could we tell the difference?

KEVIN. My back itches.

(He rubs his back against chair.)

RITA. Silence! You must not break the chain…oh, spirit world, we are trying to contact our dear departed brother, Fred Holloway. We feel his presence in this house and wish him to come forward and speak to us. *(She starts to chant.)* Ahmmm…ahmmm…

KEVIN. Rollie, scratch my back for me, will you.

ROLLIE. From here.

KEVIN. Well, why aren't you sitting next to me? You always sit next to the girls.

ROLLIE. Do not.

KEVIN. Do so.

ROLLIE. Do not!

RITA. *(normal voice)* Would you two please knock it off? The spirits are getting pissed!

(She continues to chant.)

MARTHA. What is she doing?

KEVIN. Chanting.

MARTHA. Chanting? Are we contacting ghosts or doing yoga?

RITA. Ahmmmm.

KEVIN. It's not "ahm," it's Om! Don't you even know what Om is?

RITA. *(regular voice)* Sure, Om is where the heart is.

*(**RITA** continues to chant, then faints. Two beats. Then, she awakens.)*

RITA. *(normal voice)* Did anything happen?

ROLLIE. I think my foot fell asleep.

RITA. *(normal voice)* Rats.

SAM. *(rises)* That's it. I've had enough.

MARTHA. Me too. *(She crosses, turns light on, and makes herself a drink.)*

RITA. *(chanting)* No, we must not break the spell.

ROLLIE. Would you knock it off. *(He blows out candle.)*

SAM. I told you this was nonsense.

RITA. *(back to normal voice, unless otherwise stated)* There has got to be a way. If he appeared, once he'll do it again.

ROLLIE. We're finished. Through. I'll have to hide out in South America.

RITA. Oh Rollie, can we go to Brazil? I'd love to see the Mardi Gras.

SAM. Nobody's going anywhere. I'll figure something out. Don't worry.

KEVIN. I knew I should have started a nest egg instead of putting all my money into the business. Blue chip stock and bonds. That's what I should have invested in.

SAM. That's it!

RITA. What's it?

KEVIN. Quiet, he's having another creative jag.

SAM. Why didn't I think of it before. Wall Street. We'll bring the company public. Float stock. Raise working capital!

KEVIN. *(rises)* Hello, do you hear yourself? The company's losing money hand over fist. What brokerage firm is going to bring public a stinker like this?

SAM I'll call my broker. He's with a small firm. They're hungry for new business. You fix the books a little. Amortize the losses over a few years, you know what to do to make it look better.

KEVIN. Absolutely not. I'm not going to jail for anyone.

SAM. You won't go to jail. It's done all the time. Besides, how much time would you actually serve. A few months in a country club with some other white collar criminals. When you get out, we're all flush.

KEVIN. Let Rollie do it. He's likely to wind up in jail anyway.

ROLLIE. Ha, ha.

KEVIN. Well if you helped out a little more instead of screwing around...

ROLLIE. Don't go pointing fingers at me again.

SAM. Alright you two, enough already.

MARTHA. One big happy family.

ROLLIE. Without Fred nobody can run this business.

SAM. I told you to stop bringing him up.

KEVIN. He's right, without Fred we're through.

RITA. I've got it! I've got it!

SAM. *(moving towards her)* A way to save the restaurants?

RITA. No, a way to contact Fred.

SAM. *(cups hands on ears)* I don't want to hear it.

RITA. Rollie, what were you and Kevin doing when Fred first appeared to you ten years ago?

ROLLIE. Who remembers? Playing Monopoly probably.

RITA. And what were you doing tonight?

KEVIN. *(A light comes on.)* Playing Monopoly! And every other time too?

MARTHA. Wonderful, you have a haunted Monopoly set.

RITA. Don't you see, if you all continue playing the game maybe Fred will appear again.

KEVIN. Might be worth a try.

MARTHA. There's one thing that bothers me about all of this. If Fred's been haunting you guys all these years, then how come you never thought to ask him how to save the business? We all know he was the real talent of the organization.

RITA. *(a little insulted for* **ROLLIE***)* Oh, I wouldn't say that. There is another brother who possesses charm and talent.

(She rubs **ROLLIE***'s shoulders.)*

MARTHA. That's not the kind of talent I'm referring to.

SAM. *(to* **MARTHA***)* So, now they have you believing this garbage?

MARTHA. I don't know that I believe it or not Sam, I just thought it was logical to ask.

SAM. Logical to ask? Okay Mr. Accountant, why didn't you ask the ghost his secret for success?

KEVIN. It's funny, but the first couple of years when Fred appeared it was very fast. He'd breeze past us from the bedroom and disappear into the kitchen.

ROLLIE. We didn't even acknowledge that anything strange was happening until the fourth year. We thought if we told anyone they would think we were crazy.

SAM. They do.

KEVIN. Anyway, around the fifth or sixth year, when Fred walked in, Rollie said hello to him. Fred stopped and talked, and he's stayed a little longer each year.

MARTHA. And you never discussed business?

KEVIN. Well, the whole experience is a little unnerving you know. I'm sorry if business wasn't the first thing on our minds.

RITA. Well, what did you talk about?

ROLLIE. We talked a little about Monopoly. But mostly we just talked about this house.

MARTHA. Well, if and when you ever speak to my dear departed husband again, I would suggest you ask him his advice on salvaging the Luscious Onion chain of restaurants. Oh, and one other thing, you can ask him where he hid the combination to the safe in our basement. I haven't been able to wear any of my jewelry for ten years.

RITA. That necklace you're wearing doesn't look like it came from a Cracker Jack Box.

MARTHA. Oh, this is just a bauble left over from the wedding gifts my future ex-husband didn't get his hands on.

KEVIN. *(to SAM)* Ex-husband?

SAM. I'll fill you in later.

MARTHA. Believe me, with my twenty five-percent of the business, Fred has been a better husband to me dead the last ten years than that con-artist I'm currently married to. If Fred floats in here again, ask him for help.

SAM. I can't believe what I'm hearing. Ask a phantom how to save the restaurants. Great idea! I'll tell you what, let's put him in charge of advertising. He can ghost write our ad campaigns.

ROLLIE. Can you think of anything better considering our situation?

SAM. Yes, I can mister "smooth operator." To start with, why don't you concentrate on doing one thing at a time instead of running off half cocked in all directions. You work at the restaurant, gamble, take a vacation every other week and hang out at the back room of that bar with all your poker buddies. Learn to focus.

ROLLIE. You're right Sam, you're absolutely right. I am spread too thin. I've got to take it easy before I kill myself.

SAM. Damn right.

ROLLIE. First thing tomorrow, I'm giving up working at the restaurant.

SAM. Very funny. I'm surrounded by comedians and geniuses. I'm confronted by a situation that demands action and I'm told to contact dead people by playing Monopoly!

RITA. Well, I still think it's worth a try. Rollie, Kevin: sit down and play.

(**RITA** *leads* **ROLLIE** *to the table.*)

KEVIN. Come on Sam. What have you got to lose?

SAM. I want no part of this.

MARTHA. Maybe I can find a buyer for the Luscious Onion chain that would be willing to turn them into a string of Chinese restaurants. How does the Luscious Wonton sound?

SAM. Not while I'm alive. Whose turn is it?

(*He sits at table.*)

KEVIN. Your turn, Sam.

ROLLIE. Wait, I want to build some houses.

KEVIN. You can't build houses. It's not your turn.

ROLLIE. So what, Sam's about to hit Indiana Avenue and I have the Monopoly.

KEVIN. You cannot build houses unless it's your turn, right Sam?

SAM. Who knows?

ROLLIE. I'm building. Gimmee those houses.

KEVIN. Never!

ROLLIE. Give me those houses, Kevin.

KEVIN. Not a chance in hell.

MARTHA. I can't stand to see grown men acting like children. I'm going to make some coffee.

(*She exits to kitchen.*)

ROLLIE. (*stands up*) This is the last time I'm going to ask you Kevin!

(*Fred's theme music comes up as* **FRED** *enters room.*)

FRED. Hey fella's, what's all the fighting about?

ROLLIE. Alright, alright, we'll ask him. Fred, aren't you allowed to build houses when it isn't your turn?

FRED. I don't think so, Rollie.

KEVIN. *(points finger at* **ROLLIE***)* There, you see, you see.

RITA. Who are you talking to? Wait, don't tell me...he's here, isn't he?

FRED. Hey, she's a cutie.

ROLLIE. *(a little jealous)* Layoff dead man, she's with me.

KEVIN. *(to* **ROLLIE***)* You're jealous of a ghost?

RITA. Oh, where is he, where is he?

FRED. She can't see or hear me, can she?

KEVIN. Apparently not.

*(***FRED*** slides up behind and silently mimics her during following exchange.)*

RITA. Come on, where is he? *(chanting voice)* Fred Holloway, Fred Holloway, if you are present in this room please give me a sign.

*(***FRED*** blows in her ear.)*

(she slaps **KEVIN** *who is in close proximity)* Ohhh...fresh!

ROLLIE. *(to* **FRED***)* Now, cut that out you!

FRED. Why, I'm just having some fun. I may be old but I'm not...well actually I am.

ROLLIE. You're getting a little bold now that you're gone. You know your ex-wife is still in the house.

RITA. Quiet you guys. I've had experience in this area. *(chanting again)* Fred Holloway, we want to ask you some questions. Please acknowledge by knocking once for "no" and twice for "yes."

KEVIN. That's not right. It's once for "yes" and twice for "no?"

RITA. *(normal voice)* A bit picky aren't we? *(chanting voice)* Make that once for "yes" and twice for "no." Are you here with us in this room, Fred Holloway?

FRED. *(shrugs his shoulders.)* Should I?

ROLLIE. *(back to racing form)* Humor her.

*(***FRED*** knocks once on the wall.)*

RITA. *(excited)* He hears me!

KEVIN. *(deadpan)* No kidding.

RITA. What should I ask him, what should I ask him!

ROLLIE. Ask him who he likes in the fifth race at Belmont this afternoon.

RITA. I'm being serious here. Do you want to save the restaurants or not?

KEVIN. Ask him about your recipe.

RITA. You think I should?

ROLLIE. Knock yourself out.

RITA. *(chanting)* Fred Holloway, Fred Holloway. "Rita's Rigatoni Regalé." What do you think?

(**FRED** *shrugs and gives* **ROLLIE** *questioning look.* **ROLLIE** *nods his head yes.* **FRED** *knocks once.*)

RITA. He likes the idea. I told you.

ROLLIE. Yeah, how about that.

RITA I wish there was a way I could directly communicate with him. There are so many ideas I'd like him to hear.

ROLLIE. *(stands)* I'm sure he can't wait. Come on, let's get some coffee. I'll interpret for you on the way. You coming, Fred?

(**FRED** *follows* **RITA** *and* **ROLLIE** *into the kitchen.*)

KEVIN. *(a beat)* Wait, not the kitchen! Martha's in there!

(**MARTHA** *screams offstage then wanders in dizzily.*)

MARTHA. Oh Kevin, I saw him again. Oh, I feel so faint.

(She starts to fall towards armchair.)

KEVIN. Martha, not the chair…the couch, the couch.

(She faints on couch.)

Come on, Sam. Drive me to the pharmacy. If this keeps up we're going to need smelling salts.

SAM. *(as they exit)* How did I wind up in such a nutty family? Maybe I'm adopted.

(blackout)

Scene Two

(Twenty minutes later. MARTHA is still unconscious on the couch as FRED gazes at her from near picture stage right.)

FRED. *(walking towards her)* You look great, Martha. I know you can't hear me but I just wanted to tell you that. I hope you're happy, dear. I don't even blame you for getting remarried. Oh, I was upset at first, but I know how lonely it can get when you're by yourself. You never know, Martha, someday we might be together again.

(Front door opens and RITA enters as FRED steps back into alcove. RITA walks around room, notices MARTHA, then picks up scotch bottle from bar and motions as if she were about to pour some on her, then thinks better of it and puts bottle back. She crosses to front door.)

RITA. It's okay, Rollie, the coast is clear.

ROLLIE. *(offstage)* You sure no one is around?

RITA. Nobody I care about.

ROLLIE. What do you mean?

RITA. Well, your sister-in-law is asleep on the couch again, but I don't think she'll be up anytime soon.

ROLLIE. You sure?

(RITA walks over to couch, lifts MARTHA's arm from her chest and drops it to the floor.)

RITA. Yeah, I'm sure.

ROLLIE. Okay, go ahead. You know what I want to hear.

RITA. Just a minute, I have to get ready.

(RITA positions herself on club chair with her arms and legs spread wide.)

ROLLIE. Are you ready yet?

RITA. I don't know Rollie, maybe we shouldn't, your brothers could be back any minute.

ROLLIE. I know. That's what makes it exciting. Come on already.

RITA. Okay, here goes... *(She starts flailing her arms.)* Help me, someone, help me, I'm drowning. Oh, I need some brave strong man to save me.

*(***ROLLIE*** *enters wearing bathing suit and carrying inflatable pool tube.)*

ROLLIE. I'll save you!

(He motions with his arms as if swimming towards her.)

RITA. *(She stands up next to chair with her back towards* **ROLLIE.** *)* Oh my, a strong handsome lifeguard is coming to my rescue.

(As she delivers next line, she flails her arm again and accidentally hits **ROLLIE** *in the nose, and he falls unconscious to club chair.)*

Please, save me my...oh , oh Rollie! Speak to me, speak to me!

*(***KEVIN*** *and* **SAM** *come through front door.)*

SAM. What the heck is going on now?

KEVIN. Now, there's two of them!

*(***KEVIN*** *is carrying washcloth and starts alternating wagging it under* **MARTHA***'s and* **ROLLIE***'s noses.)*

RITA. We had a little accident.

*(***ROLLIE*** *starts to come to as* **FRED** *walks over.)*

RITA. Oh, Rollie, Rollie, speak to me, where does it hurt?

ROLLIE. My nose, my nose.

RITA. Oh my, it's swollen. I'll get you some ice.

FRED. Hold your head back, Rollie.

ROLLIE. Shut up you, I don't need your advice.

RITA. *(insulted)* Well, I'm only trying to help.

SAM. Yeah, quit picking on her.

ROLLIE. I wasn't picking on her.

RITA. Put your head back, sweetie.

FRED. Maybe there's ointment in the medicine chest.

ROLLIE. Would you shut up already.

RITA. That does it, I'm not gonna stand around here and be insulted.

(She exits to kitchen in a huff.)

KEVIN. Nice going, Rollie.

ROLLIE. You know I wasn't talking to her.

SAM. Then who were you talking to?

FRED. I didn't mean to upset you, Rollie.

ROLLIE. Can't you go haunt someone else?

(MARTHA comes to and KEVIN helps her to her feet. She turns and sees FRED.)

FRED. Hi, Martha.

(She faints back on couch.)

SAM. What happened to her?

KEVIN. *(to FRED)* Would you please go away.

SAM. Okay, if that's the way you feel, I'll be in the kitchen with, Rita.

(He exits.)

FRED. Gee, fellas, I'm awfully sorry.

KEVIN. It's not your fault Fred. Where Rollie goes trouble follows.

ROLLIE. That's right, kick me when I'm down.

KEVIN. It's your gambling and spending. Will you ever get your financial life in order?

ROLLIE. Again with the lecture.

KEVIN. Have you made the alimony payments to your ex-wife?

ROLLIE. I'm a little behind.

KEVIN. What's a little?

ROLLIE. Eight or nine months.

FRED. Gee, Rollie, she could throw you in jail.

KEVIN. Is there a reward if I turn him in?

ROLLIE. If there was a reward, I'd turn myself in.

FRED. I wish you guys would stop fighting all the time.

ROLLIE. You keep out of it. Some ghost, the only person you can scare is your ex-wife.

FRED. That's not true.

ROLLIE. Oh yeah, how come Rita and Sam can't see you?

KEVIN. Quit picking on him, Rollie.

FRED. Sam sees me, he just won't admit it.

ROLLIE. Yeah, what about Rita?

FRED. Now don't make me angry, Rollie.

(Music comes on and front door swings open.)

KEVIN. Yeah, don't make him angry, Rollie.

ROLLIE. He doesn't scare me with his music and doors. All he is, is a pest, that's all. Why don't you appear to Rita, you can compare recipes, at least that would be something useful.

KEVIN. Don't listen to him, Fred. He doesn't mean it, he's under a lot of pressure.

FRED. Oh yeah, Rollie, oh yeah. I'll show you who I can scare.

(He's off to kitchen.)

KEVIN. You had to go upset him again didn't you. You know what you are Rollie?

ROLLIE. No what am I?

KEVIN. You're nothing but a bully, that's what you are.

ROLLIE. Sure, sure, you always took his side, dead or alive.

KEVIN. He's sensitive. Always was. He's not a street guy like you.

ROLLIE. Let me get my violin. *(beat)* Look, Kevin, I'm in real trouble this time, the guys I owe money to play rough.

KEVIN. Well it's your own fault, and then you drag that poor woman into it.

(RITA screams offstage.)

KEVIN. Now what?

(SAM enters.)

SAM. Get in here you two!

ROLLIE. What happened?

SAM. Your girlfriend fainted, that's what happened. Kevin, bring the smelling salts.

ROLLIE. How'd it happen?

SAM. One minute I'm standing there talking to her, then she screams and faints. Come on.

(SAM, ROLLIE and KEVIN run to kitchen to attend to RITA as FRED enters from bedroom entrance. On the couch, MARTHA starts to moan and recover as FRED approaches her.)

FRED. Martha, can you hear me? Don't be frightened, it's me, Fred.

MARTHA. *(puts hand to head)* Oh, Fred.

FRED. Please don't faint again Martha, I won't hurt you. I just want to talk to you.

MARTHA. Okay. I'm okay.

FRED. Good.

MARTHA. Fred, what are you doing here? How is this possible?

FRED. I don't know, Martha, all I know is I'm here.

MARTHA. Yes, you are, aren't you.

FRED. I missed you, Martha.

MARTHA. I missed you, too, Fred. I missed you terribly.

FRED. Was it hard for you Martha? You know after I was gone?

MARTHA. What do you think Fred. That terrible night. We all waited for you to come back from the ocean and you never did. You just...never did. At first I was upset. And later on angry.

FRED. At whom?

MARTHA. You, for going swimming that night. Myself, for not stopping you.

(She paces the room.)

You know I always loved staying at this house with you. It was our little romantic getaway. The evenings we spent cuddled by the fire, just listening to the waves breaking on the beach.

FRED. I remember. And how about the parties we'd have here with the boys, and the annual summer talent show at the volunteer firehouse?

MARTHA. Yes. Your night to shine. The shy introspective chef became the master of ceremonies.

FRED. Remember the sign I used to give you from the stage at the curtain call. The one that meant I loved you.

MARTHA. I do. *(She beats her hand gently against her heart.)* I loved this place Fred. But ever since that terrible night, I couldn't come back here. Until tonight.

FRED. I'm sorry everything happened the way it did.

MARTHA. So am I, Fred. And it is good to see you again. If I really am seeing you and not just dreaming all of this.

SAM. *(from offstage)* She's coming to. Let's get her to the couch.

FRED. I'd better go. I don't want to frighten Rita again. Would you do me a favor, Martha?

MARTHA. If I can Fred.

FRED. Would you try and help the boys out if you can?

MARTHA. Sure. If I can.

FRED. I'm going to sit in Mom's bedroom and look out at her garden. It always cheered me up.

MARTHA. Goodbye, Fred.

FRED. Goodbye, Martha

(FRED exits to bedroom as ROLLIE and KEVIN help RITA onto the couch as SAM follows.)

ROLLIE. Lay down here, babe. Are you okay now?

RITA. I'm a little better.

SAM. What happened to her?

ROLLIE. What do you think happened, she saw Fred.

SAM. She did not. It's impossible.

MARTHA. I wouldn't be so sure. I saw him too.

SAM. I've heard just about enough of this.

(heading for front door)

KEVIN. Where are you going?

SAM. For a walk on the beach. And then to bed!

(He exits.)

ROLLIE. I better go with him.

(He exits.)

RITA. Boy, this couch is lumpy. I think I'll go to bed.

(getting up)

(to KEVIN*)* Which bedroom should I use?

KEVIN. Use my parent's room, it has the most comfortable mattress. End of the hall, to the left.

RITA. Thanks. Goodnight.

(She exits.)

MARTHA. Your parent's bedroom? I wouldn't have done that.

KEVIN. Why not?

*(*RITA *screams offstage.)*

KEVIN. So, they'll exchange recipes.

MARTHA. Well, I guess I'll turn in too. How about you, Kev?

KEVIN. Not just yet. I told Susan I'd call in the morning, but maybe I'll just give her a ring tonight.

(looking at his watch)

I hope she's still up.

MARTHA. Suit yourself. I'll see you tomorrow.

(exits to bedroom)

KEVIN. *(takes cell phone from pocket and dials number)* Hello, this is Kevin, who's this? The plumber, at this time of night? The dishwasher's broke, huh? May I speak to Mrs. Holloway please? *(surprise)* Susan, *(abruptly)* my wife! Thank you. *(pause)* Hi Susan, it's me, Kevin. *(more abruptly)* Your husband! What's the plumber doing there at this time of night? *(pause)* The toilet's backed up? I thought it was the dishwasher? Oh, the toilet backed up into the dishwasher, huh? Remind

me to eat off the paper plates tomorrow. How are
the kids? They're not home?! You mean you and Mr.
Drano are home all alone at eleven thirty at night?!
(pause) I realize he's cleaning your pipes, that's what
I'm worried about! So, where "are" the kids. They're
at your mother's? *(pause)* She says Amanda's throwing
up again? *(pause)* Sure, I'll drop by the pharmacy on
the way home tomorrow morning, ah, do you think
the plumber will be done by then? Uh-huh. By the
way, what is all this costing me, are you paying him by
the hour or is he charging a night differential? *(pause)*
Eventually, it's going to cost me plenty, I thought as
much. *(pause)* You gotta go, huh? Okay, see you tomorrow.

*(He puts away phone and crosses to bar to make a
drink.)*

(yells to bedroom) Martha, I think I'm going to need the
name of you're divorce lawyer.

(downs a scotch)

DELICIOUS!

(exits to bedroom)

(blackout)

Scene Three

(The next afternoon. Suitcases are packed and placed near front door. **SAM** *is seated on couch next to* **MARTHA**.*)*

SAM. So, that's it then, Martha. The end of an era. No more Holloway's in the restaurant business.

*(***FRED*** *stands in the doorway unnoticed.)*

MARTHA. I'm afraid I don't see any other way Sam.

SAM. Seventy years, Martha. Seventy years we've had those restaurants in the family. My grandfather started with a hot dog stand on Route 9 and since then, well you know... I tried, Martha, I tried my best not to lose them but...

MARTHA. I know you did, Sam.

SAM. It's just a shame.

MARTHA. You know, Sam, coming back to this house, all the happy memories. I really had great times here with your family, everyone always treated me more like a sister than a sister-in-law, and well, seeing him again, I just...

(She sees **FRED** *in doorway and gives him a quick smile.)*

SAM. What are you trying to say, Martha?

MARTHA. Sam, if you should find another buyer for this house soon, I want you to take my share of the proceeds, and use it to try and save the Luscious Onion. Give it one last shot.

SAM. You really mean that, Martha.

MARTHA. Yes, I really mean it. Hell, I might even move back east and help you run them.

SAM. I couldn't think of anyone I'd rather work with, but Martha, you're broke. What will you live on in the mean time?

MARTHA. Don't worry about me, I'll land on my feet. It's funny but last night the combination to the safe in my basement suddenly came back to me.

(She looks at **FRED**, *kisses* **SAM** *on the cheek, rises, goes to door and picks up her bag)*

Say goodbye to the boys for me. I'll be in touch.

(She looks at **FRED**, *places her hand to her heart and gives him the signal which he returns in kind. She exits.)*

*(***SAM*** *rises and crosses to picture, he is looking at it as* **RITA** *enters from kitchen.)*

RITA. All packed, Sam?

SAM. Oh, yes. Yes, I am. And how are you this morning young lady?

RITA. Just wonderful thank you. I took a walk on the beach with Rollie this morning. It's such a glorious day.

SAM. Yes, it is, isn't it?

RITA. It's a shame you're going to have to close the Luscious Onion. I really enjoyed working there.

SAM. Now, don't go jumping the gun. I've got a feeling the Luscious Onion chain will be around for quite a few years yet.

RITA. That *would* be glorious.

SAM. Roland and I were talking last night and he told me all about you. Seems you've got quite creative touch. He showed me a list of ideas you gave him last night that sound terrific. I'd like to transfer you to headquarters and have you try them out as my assistant.

RITA. Oh, Mr. Holloway, that sounds wonderful.

SAM. Please Rita, call me Sam.

(She hugs him.)

RITA. Oh, it's just so wonderful, Sam.

SAM. But tell me something, where did you come up with all those great ideas?

RITA. *(walks to picture)* Let's just say I have a silent partner.

(winks at **FRED***)*

SAM. Is that so?

RITA. Oh, I can't wait to tell Rollie.

SAM. Don't worry, he already knows. By the way, about my brother, you seem like a very perceptive person. I think you realize that Rollie is not exactly marriage material.

RITA. I know, but he'll still be a lot of fun to work with. *(reassuringly)* Don't worry Sam, I won't get too attached, I promise.

SAM. That's the spirit. After all, you're a great looking gal. Find yourself a nice guy to settle down with, like Kevin and Susan.

RITA. I don't know that Kevin is the prime example of wedded bliss, but I get your drift.

SAM. By the way, where are my brothers?

RITA. They got a call from the local real estate agent this morning who said he might have some interest in the house, so the boys ran down there. It's been awhile since they left. I wonder what's keeping them?

SAM. If I know Rollie, he took a detour to Aqueduct.

(Door fly's open and SAM and ROLLIE come in.)

ROLLIE. Good news Sammy boy, I think we've got ourselves a buyer.

SAM. That's terrific. You think it's for real. And soon.

KEVIN. They seemed very anxious in this prime bit of beach property.

ROLLIE. Come on everyone. We'll talk about it over lunch, it's on…

(Again ROLLIE searches in empty pockets and gives KEVIN a look.)

KEVIN. Me. Come on, I'm buying lunch.

(They all exit except SAM who lingers to look at picture.)

ROLLIE. *(reenters)* Come on, Sammy.

SAM. Wait in the car, I'll be right there, I just want to take a last look around.

ROLLIE. Okay. Don't be long.

(He exits.)

(SAM picks up Monopoly game from the table and heads for the door, then turns and puts the game back on the table.)

SAM. It belongs with the house

(*He starts for the door once more.*)

FRED. (*steps from doorway*) Goodbye, Sam.

SAM. (*His back is to* **FRED.**) You're not real.

FRED. Then how come you answered me? You can hear me, can't you Sam?

(**SAM** *turns slowly.*)

SAM. Yes, I can hear you.

FRED. And you can see me too, can't you?

SAM. Yes. I can see you.

FRED. All these years?

SAM. Yes, all these years.

FRED. Then why didn't you ever talk to me Sam?

SAM. Why? Why? Because, I thought if I did, I'd admit to myself I was insane. That's why.

FRED. You were scared?

SAM. Yes, I was scared…and sorry.

FRED. For what?

SAM. For everything. For giving you that night off ten years ago.

FRED. It wasn't your fault, Sam. It was an accident.

SAM. Pop left me in charge, don't you understand. You were older than me but Pop left me in charge.

FRED. I didn't want to run the business, Sam. You knew that. Pop knew that. I was more valuable in the kitchen than the office.

SAM. I know that but you were still my responsibility…*my* responsibility.

FRED. Sam, a person is only responsible for his own actions. You didn't force me to go swimming that night. Don't you see that?

SAM. No, I don't.

FRED. Stop beating yourself up, Sam. You're my brother, I love you. I'll always love you.

SAM. That's why you haunt me like this?

FRED. I'll tell you what, Sam. I'll make you a deal. I'll try to keep a low profile around here, if you'll do something in return.

SAM. What could I possibly do for you?

FRED. Take the money from this house and go save the Luscious Onion. And give that Rita a chance. She's got a pretty good head on her shoulders.

SAM. You got yourself a deal kiddo.

*(**ROLLIE** re-enters room.)*

ROLLIE. Sam, would you come on, everyone's waiting.

SAM. I'm coming, I'm coming. *(to **FRED**)* Goodbye, Freddy.

ROLLIE. Yeah, goodbye kid. Uh, you gonna be okay?

FRED. What can happen to me?

ROLLIE. Yeah, you've got a point.

*(They exit. **FRED** is alone on stage. Two beats then three gunshots are heard offstage. **RITA** screams. The others utter comments offstage such as "call the police" or "**ROLLIE**'s been shot.")*

RITA. *(screams offstage)* Rollie, oh Rollie. Someone call an ambulance!

*(A beat. Fred's theme music starts playing, lights flicker then come up and **ROLLIE** enters.)*

FRED. Rollie, what happened?

ROLLIE. Can you believe it, kid? That bastard Johnny Simms! He came out of nowhere and fired three shots at me. It's a good thing he missed, and I ducked back in here. I could have been killed. I need a drink.

(As he turns his back to audience he reveals three bullet holes in the back of his jacket.)

FRED. Did you say could of been killed?

ROLLIE. *(stops and goes back to **FRED**)* Yeah, why?

FRED. I got news for you buddy, take a look at the back of your jacket.

(ROLLIE removes his jacket and holds it out so the back is visible to himself and audience.)

ROLLIE. Nah, it couldn't be…could it?

RITA. *(offstage)* Oh, Rollie, he was so young. How could he die like this?

FRED. It sure could.

ROLLIE. But it can't be. I've got things to do, places to see. Sam was gonna give Rita a bonus, so I could take her to Bermuda.

FRED. Not anymore.

ROLLIE. But I got a hot tip on a sure thing running at Belmont this afternoon.

FRED. Sorry pal, your luck just ran out. It's just too bad you didn't have life insurance or something.

ROLLIE. Who said I didn't? When you travel in my circles, you cover all your bases. I may have been irresponsible, but I wasn't stupid.

FRED. How much were you covered for?

ROLLIE. A million-dollar key-man term life with double indemnity for accidental death or foul play. Kevin got it for me.

FRED. Nice. Who's the beneficiary?

ROLLIE. The Luscious Onion restaurants. Poor Kevin and Sam, how are they ever going to run the business without my help?

FRED. Two million dollars, huh? I think they'll manage okay without you. You know, I always knew you had a heart under that tough exterior. Pop would have been proud.

ROLLIE. Thanks, kid.

FRED. What do we do know?

ROLLIE. You got me, I'm new at this racket.

FRED. You get used to it. So who'd you wind up selling the house to?

ROLLIE. The local college bought it. They're going to turn it into a sorority house. I think they're gonna study oceanography or something.

FRED. Sorority house, huh, college girls?

ROLLIE. Yeah, I guess we could haunt them for a little while.

FRED. I guess. What do we do in the meantime?

ROLLIE. How about a game of Monopoly?

FRED. Sounds good to me.

(They walk towards the table.)

FRED. I'm the racing car.

ROLLIE. No, I'm the racing car.

FRED. I was here first.

ROLLIE. But, I'm the youngest.

FRED. I'm the senior ghost.

(Adlibs continue as curtain closes.)

(curtain)

COSTUME PLOT

SAM: Act 1, scene 1 – Hawaiian shirt, straw hat and khakis.

Other scenes – casual attire

KEVIN: Act 1, scene 1 – business suit

Other scenes – casual attire

ROLLIE: Casual attire

Act 2, scene 2 – bathing suit

RITA: tight dresses and blouses

Act 2, scene 2 – bathing suit

FRED: casual attire

MARTHA: Act 1, scene2 – business casual

Other scenes – casual

PERSONAL PROPS

ROLLIE: Racing form, shaving kit, rubber floatation device
SAM: Ukelele, Monopoly set
KEVIN: Brief case, smelling salts

GENERAL PROPS

Picture of Beach house (rigged to fall off wall)

Luggage

HEAVEN HELP ME

Stage Schematic

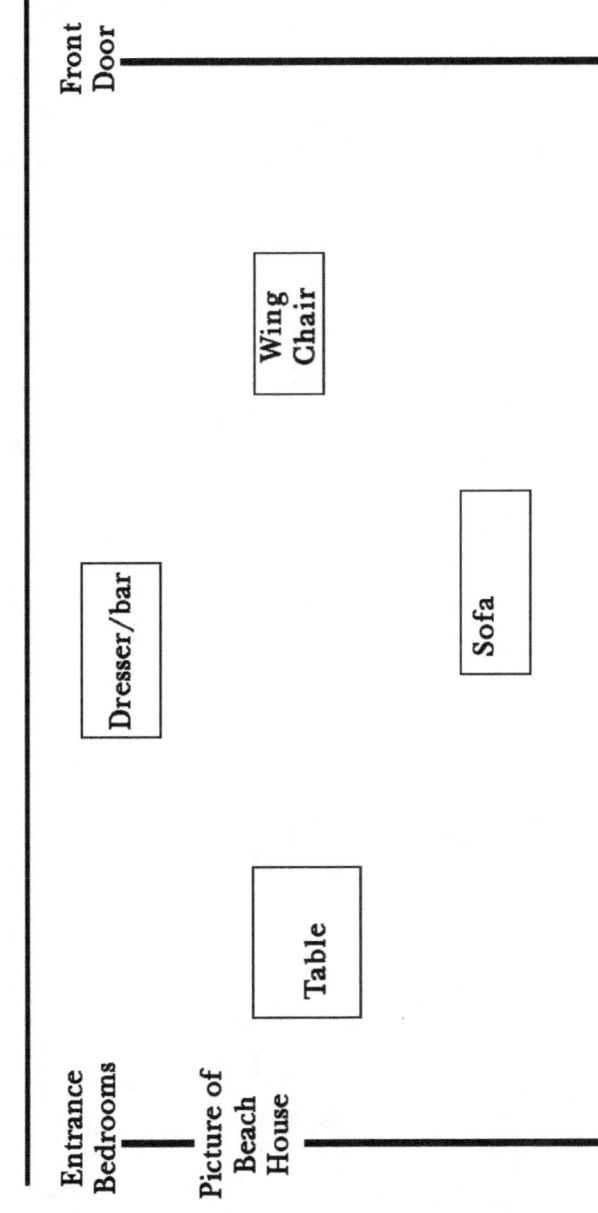